CONTENTS

(c) 1997 Viacom International Inc. All Rights Reserved. Nickelodeon, Rugrats and all related titles, logos and characters are trademarks of Viacom International Inc. Created by Klasky - Csupo, Inc. Published in Great Britain 1997 by World International Limited, Deanway Technology Centre, Wilmslow Road, Handforth, Cheshire, SK9 3FB
Printed in Italy ISBN 0 7498 3394 7

£5.50
UK Only

The Race Is On

Grandpa has left out a bottle of chocolate milk as a treat for Tommy, but everyone wants to get their hands on it!
Follow the key and trace along the tangled lines, adding the seconds as you go. Who got to drink the milk first?
The answer is at the bottom of the page.

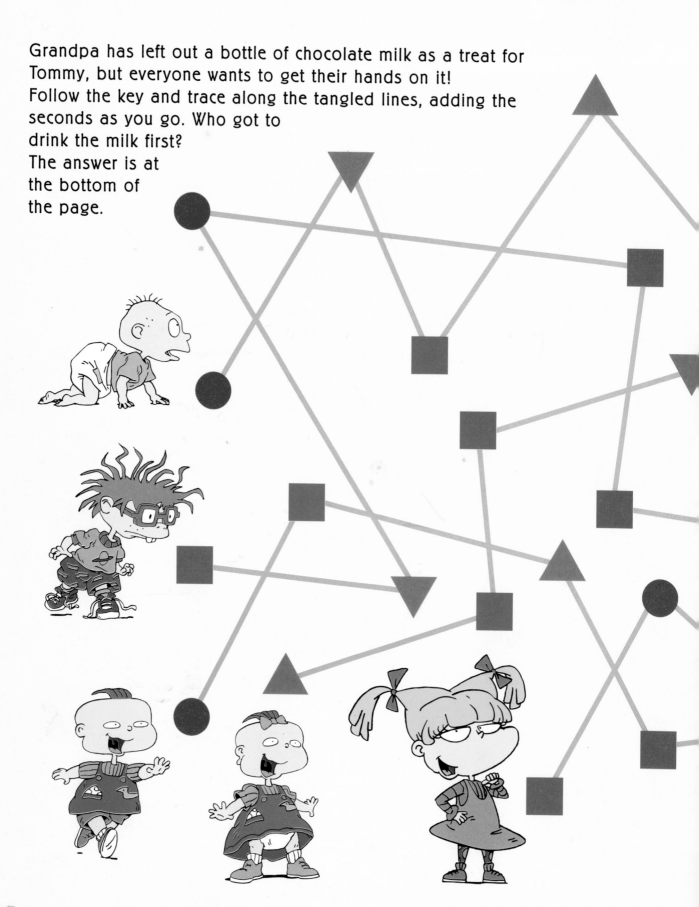

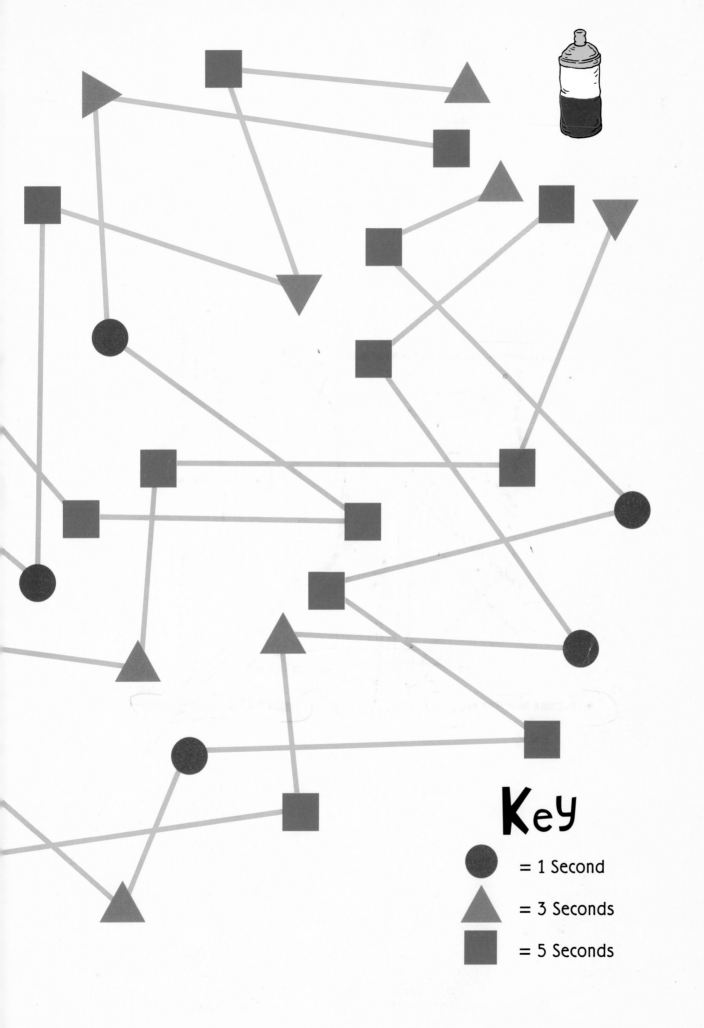

Key

● = 1 Second

▲ = 3 Seconds

■ = 5 Seconds

Animal Wordsearch

Can you help the Rugrats to find the creatures' names listed below, hidden in the wordsearch?

The words appear across, down, up and diagonally! When you have completed the wordsearch, the remaining letters spell a message!

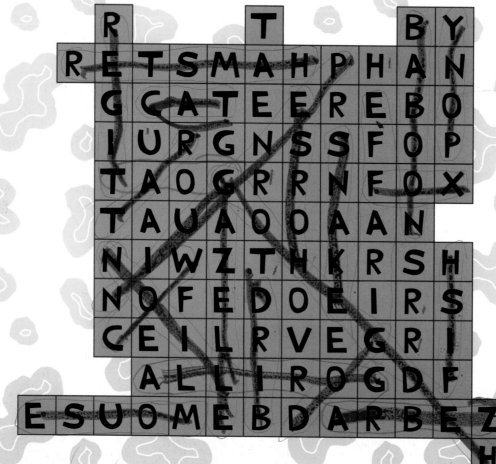

```
R        T        B Y
R E T S M A H P H A N
G C A T E E R E B O
I U R G N S S F O P
T A O G R R N F O X
T A U A O O A A N
N I W Z T H K R S H
N O F E D O E I R S
C E I L R V E G R I
A L L I R O G D F
E S U O M E B D A R B E Z
                      H
```

COW ✓
GORILLA ✓
TIGER ✓
ZEBRA ✓
RAT ✓
HAMSTER
HORSE ✓
SNAKE

PENGUIN ✓
LION ✓
BABOON ✓
PONY ✓
GOAT ✓
FISH ✓
FOX

MOUSE ✓
GAZELLE ✓
BIRD ✓
HEDGEHOG ✓
DOG ✓
GIRAFFE ✓
CAT ✓

Chuckie's Imaginary Friend

Tommy and the twins were bored just sitting in their playpen. Then the doorbell rang.

"Hi, Charles! Hi, Chuckie!" said Didi, opening the door.

"Hi, Didi! I'm re-labelling my self-help video tapes," said Charles. "Have you got any spare stick-on labels?"

"**W**anna know what I been up to, guys?" asked Chuckie, as Charles followed Didi into the kitchen.

Before anyone had time to answer, Chuckie went on, "It's really a secret, so maybe I better not talk about it."

"Come on, Chuckie...tell us!" said Tommy.

"Well...I got this new friend," smiled Chuckie. "His name's Barney...and we been doin' lots of neat stuff together!"

"Like what?" asked Tommy.

"Yesterday, we hid under my dad's bed...and before that, we crawled into that creepy space under the front porch," Chuckie grinned.

"Wow! Weren't you scared?" asked Lil.

"Nah! With Barney around, I'm not afraid of anythin'!" said Chuckie.

"What's he look like?" asked Tommy.

"Well..." said Chuckie, hesitating. "Well...he, he kinda looks like me!"

"Maybe he can come over and play!" suggested Tommy.

"He, um...lives kinda far away in this...uh...castle place and...he's not allowed to cross the street!" Chuckie mumbled, hoping that the others would start talking about something else.

Just then, Charles and Didi came into the living-room.

"Too bad you've only got red labels, Didi," sighed Charles. "I really need brown ones...to match my other ones."

"Say, Chaz, Betty talked me into running in the 'Save the Grunion' race tomorrow. D'you mind taking the kids?" asked Didi.

"No problem, Didi. They can come over to my house," said Charles.

"Did you hear that?" whispered Tommy. "We're goin' over to Chuckie's tomorrow!"

Good luck at the race!" called Charles, when Didi and Betty dropped off Tommy and the twins.

"PSSSSST!" hissed Chuckie. "I got somethin' to show you guys!"

Chuckie bravely led Tommy and the twins into the long, dark hallway.

What a creepy place!" gulped Phil, as Chuckie took them on into a messy bedroom.

"Does a monster live in here?" asked Tommy.

"Nah, just my dad," said Chuckie.

At the other end of the room, Chuckie opened a door leading to another dark room.

"I come in here with Barney to look at scary things...like that!" said Chuckie. He shone a flashlight on to his dad's plaque of a huge, bug-eyed fish!

"Say, w-where is Barney?" gulped Tommy, looking around the room.
"Well, uh...it's very sad. Barney wouldn't eat his broccoli...so they sent him to prism!" Chuckie blushed.

"Hey, Chuckie said if Barney gets outta prism, they're gonna go to the park tomorrow!" grinned Tommy, as he and the twins drove home.
"Yeah?" said Phil.
"Well, I got a idea!" whispered Tommy.

"While Didi soaked her aching feet in a bowl of water, Tommy fetched his bucket and spade.
"Aw, Tommy, I'm too tired to take you out now," groaned Didi. But when Tommy looked out of the window and waved his little spade in the air, Didi gave in - and took him to the park!

"...and the back of the closet was one thing, but the moon? How d'ya get to the moon?" asked Chuckie, as he sat on a grassy mound in the park.
Pushing some bushes aside, Tommy looked to see who Chuckie was with, then gasped. There was no one else there!
"Who're you talking to, Chuckie?" asked Tommy, coming out of the bush.
"Um...well...I was talking to...Barney!" replied Chuckie.
"I don't see anyone!" said Tommy.
"That's because Barney is invisdible!" Chuckie explained.

9

"Barney, I'd like you to meet Tommy," Chuckie went on.

"Hi, Barney," said Tommy, puzzled.

"Barney's um, kinda shy. He only talks to me," Chuckie explained.

"But..." Tommy began.

"Time to go, Tommykins!" called Didi.

Back home, Tommy was telling the twins about Chuckie's friend, when Charles and Chuckie arrived.

"I got to thinking about my tapes, Didi...and well, I could use those red labels for my nature documentaries!" said Charles.

"Barney...meet my friends!" smiled Chuckie, as Charles and Didi left the room.

"What neat things does Barney want to do, Chuckie?" asked Phil.

"Ummmm, I'll ask him," stammered Chuckie. "Er, Barney, what do you think we should do?"

"Well?" said Tommy, at last.

"He's thinking!" said Chuckie. "What, Barney?...Uh-huh...that's a great idea!"

"What's he say, Chuckie?" asked Phil.

"Guys, ya ever wonder what's under the rug?" asked Chuckie, slyly.

Tommy, Phil, Lil and Chuckie crawled under the rug and felt around.

"What'd you guys find?" asked Tommy.

"Barney 'n' me found this penny!" laughed Chuckie.

"I found this great big piece o' dust!" said Tommy. "I'm gonna save it and see if it keeps growing!"

"What does Barney think we should do now?" sighed Tommy, when Didi put him and the other babies into their playpen.
"Um...Barney says he doesn't have any ideas," Chuckie mumbled.
"I don't think you're asking him right!" said Phil.

Chuckie struggled to think of something. "Okay...Barney has an idea!" he said at last. "He thinks...we should go on the roof!"
"How're we gonna get to the roof?" asked Phil.

Tommy had a plan. He led the Rugrats into Grandpa's bedroom and pointed to some stairs leading up to the attic.
"Maybe this isn't such a good idea," said Chuckie.
"Barney says it is!" said Phil.

Flustered, Chuckie gasped, "Wait! What did ya say, Barney? Yeah?...Yeah?...Barney thinks we better go back downstairs!"
"Does Barney say we should go back, or do you say we should go back?" asked Phil, suspiciously.

STOP!" cried Chuckie, as Tommy climbed the stairs. "This is not a good idea!"
"Barney says it is!" called Tommy.
"Barney's wrong!" spluttered Chuckie, trying to hold Tommy back.
"But Barney's never wrong!" said Lil.
"He is this time!" said Chuckie.
"How d'ya know?" asked Tommy.
"Because...because Barney isn't real!" sobbed Chuckie, sitting down on the stairs. "I-I just made him up!"

"So all that brave stuff Barney did, like going in your dad's closet and taking us under the rug...that was you?" gasped Tommy. "Yeah, it was just me," sighed Chuckie. Then he realised just how brave he'd been. "Hey, it was me!" Chuckie laughed.

"Say, Chuckie, can you bring Barney back?" asked Lil, a little later.
"Nah, once you say a guy's made up, it's kinda hard to get him to come over anymore," said Chuckie.
"Time to go, Chuckie," called Charles.
"I'm bored!" sighed Phil, as Chuckie and his dad went out the door. "I'm more bored than you, Philip!" said Lil.

"Just wait there, Chuckie, I've forgotten the stick-on labels!" said Charles, racing back into the house.
"I'm sorry I told that fib about you bein' made up, Barney," whispered

Chuckie, as he stood in the front garden. "But from now on, maybe it would be better if we didn't tell other people about you, huh?" Smiling, Chuckie went on, "Oh yeah, Barney...you'll always be my friend, too!"

12

AMAZING ANIMAL FACTS!

Grandpa told the Rugrats some very strange but true things about different animals.

"I wonder if Angelica would sing if she rubbed her legs together?" Tommy whispered to Chuckie, when Grandpa told them about grasshoppers.

Here are some other amazing animal facts from Grandpa!

Grasshoppers sing by rubbing their legs together!

Squirrels use their tails like parachutes. They have been seen falling from trees as high as a 50-storey building, without hurting themselves!

A thread from a spider's web is as strong as steel of the same thickness!

An ant can lift a weight 50 times heavier than itself – and pull a branch 300 times heavier than itself!

Swifts can fly non-stop for years at a time! They eat, drink and even sleep in the air!

If a cat has one litter, that litter could reproduce more than 20,000 cats in just two years!

Although kangaroos can be as large as humans, a newborn kangaroo is only 1 centimetre long!

Frogs can jump over 100 times their own length! If you could jump as well as a frog, you could leap over at least one football pitch!

Fleas are even better jumpers! If you could jump as well as a flea, you could leap over the length of four football pitches – and as high as a 60-storey building!

13

Which Rugrat Are You Most Like?

Are you adventurous, curious - and a born leader, like Tommy? yes
Are you bossy - someone who loves to show-off, like
Angelica? Or are you a 'fraidy-cat' who can see danger
lurking everywhere, just like Chuckie? Answer these funny
questions, then check your score at the bottom of the
page to find out who you're really like!

Q1: Your dad leaves a big box on a table. Inside, something is scratching and moving around. Would you...

a) Scream your head off and hide from the 'monster'?

b) Feel nervous, but peek inside the box anyway? ✓

c) Think it might be something you can scare your friends with?

Q2: Your Auntie and Uncle are staying for the weekend. Do you...

a) Try to impress them with your singing and dancing?

b) Hope they won't want to do anything too exciting?

c) Hope they'll want to do something really exciting? ✓

Q3: Your best friend doesn't understand how to play a game. Would you...

a) Patiently show him how to play the game - several times? ✓

b) Tell him he's a 'big baby' who doesn't understand anything?

c) Burst into tears and say you can't play the game, either?

Q4: If your mum and dad took you to a safari park, would you...

a) Spend the whole day trying to hide inside your dad's jacket?

b) Tell everyone you can run faster than any cheetah?

c) Hope the lions come right up to your car? ✓

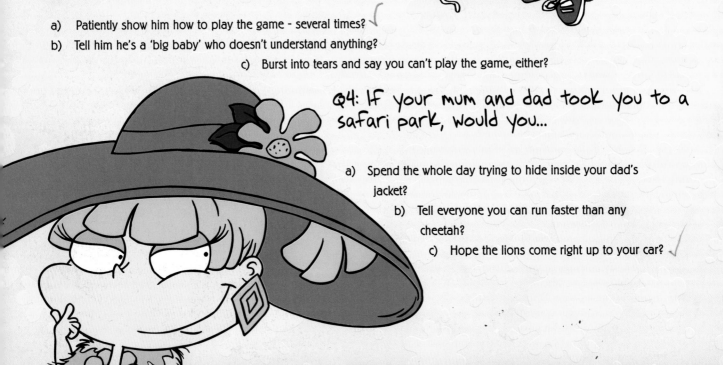

Q5: Which of these books would you most like...

a) A book about witches who cast spells and turn babies into frogs?

b) An exciting adventure book? ✓

c) A book of nursery rhymes?

Q6: You've only one Reptar bar left. Would you...

a) Share it with your friend? ✓

b) Cry because you thought you had more?

c) Wave the Reptar bar under your friend's nose - then eat it quickly?

Q7: You've been given a new kite for your birthday, so do you...

a) Hold on tightly to the string in case the kite carries you away? ✓

b) Complain that the kite isn't as big as some you've seen?

c) Run as fast as you can, pulling the kite behind you?

Q8 You can invite as many friends as you like to your birthday party. Do you...

a) Invite hundreds of children, because then you'll get hundreds of presents?

b) Invite hundreds of children, because then it will be even more fun? ✓

c) Invite just a few very close friends, because you're scared of crowds?

Who are you most like?

If you scored 6 to 12...
BOO! Did that scare ya, huh? That's 'cos you're a bit of a 'fraidy cat...like Chuckie! Swat away those scary thoughts and be more like Tommy!

If you scored 13 to 18...
You're definitely like Tommy...the leader of the gang and always in search of excitement! But don't get too bossy...or you'll turn into Angelica!

If you scored 19 to 24...
Angelica had better watch out - it looks like she has a rival! But you can't be bossy and have friends. If you want to be really popular, take a few tips from Tommy!

Check your score! 1. a (1), b (2), c (3). 2. a (3), b (1), c (2). 3. a (2), b (3), c (1). 4. a (1), b (3), c (2). 5. a (3), b (2), c (1). 6. a (3), b (1), c (2). 7. a (1), b (3), c (2). 8. a (3), b (2), c (1).

15

Long-lasting Sandcastles

The Rugrats were having a great time, until they all wanted to play with the same toy!

"I sawed Tommy's Reptar first, Lillian!" cried Phil.
"Did not!" cried Lil.
"Did too!" scowled Phil.

"It doesn't matter who sawed it first," bawled Chuckie. "Please stop shouting, 'cos it scares me!"
"Now look what've you've done! You've made Chuckie cry!" said Tommy.

"Phillip shouted first!" said Lil.

"Did not!" sulked Phil.

"Did too!" gasped Lil.

"Come on, guys!" smiled Tommy. "Let's all go into the garden and play in my sandpit."

Tommy ran as fast as he could - and landed in the sandpit with a THUD!

"Ouch! That hurt!" gasped Tommy. Nearly all the sand had disappeared from the pit!

Just then, Stu and Drew came into the garden and lifted sacks of sand off the ground and put them into a wheelbarrow.

"The sand in Tommy's sandpit was dirty and needed changing, so I had an idea," explained Stu. "I'm going to mix this sand with cement and use it to make a paved area in the front garden."

As Stu and Drew pushed the wheelbarrow through to the front garden, Chuckie's dad came along.

"You'll have to stop playing now, Chuckie. It's time for your lunch!" he called.

Chuckie didn't want to stop playing with his friends, and burst into tears as Chaz scooped him up and carried him down the garden path! Just then, a truck arrived outside the Pickles' house. Stu and Drew puffed and panted as they lifted heavy sacks off the back of the truck and put them next to the sacks of sand.

"I'm not sure I like the idea of a paved area," said Didi, as Stu dug over part of the front lawn. "In fact, I think it will look too plain and...and too bare!"

"It'll look wonderful, Deed!" smiled Stu, who thought that anything would be better than having to mow the lawn!

After lunch, Chuckie came back to play with Tommy and the twins.

"Every night, my mom sits me in the tub and says, 'I'll soon make you a nice clean boy again'!" said Tommy.

"So?" said Chuckie, looking puzzled.

"'So...my dad said the sand needs cleaning. If we can be washed clean, so can sand!" grinned Tommy. "Then we can put the sand back in my sandpit!" The Rugrats used seaside buckets and spades, plastic beakers and their hands, to take the 'sand' out of the sacks and put it in a huge pile on the driveway.

The Rugrats can't read, so they couldn't see that some of the sacks had 'CEMENT' written on them!

"Now turn on the tap!" called Tommy, as he and Chuckie struggled to hold on to the hosepipe.

"Turn the tap, Phillip!" gasped Lil.

"I'm trying, Lillian!" puffed Phil.

"Try harder then, Phillip!" panted Lil.

Suddenly, the tap turned - and water whooshed out of the hose!

"Not so fast!" spluttered Tommy, as the hosepipe did a funny, wriggly dance. Still holding on, Tommy and Chuckie were pulled to and fro on the lawn!

"Th-that thing's alive! It's a wiggly snake!" sobbed Chuckie.

"Don't cry, Chuckie. It's only a silly old hosepipe," said Tommy, as water dripped off his clothes and formed a puddle at his feet.

"I don't want to play this washing game anymore, Tommy!" sniffed Chuckie, who only stopped crying when Tommy promised him first go in his clean sandpit.

At last, Tommy, Chuckie and the twins managed to 'wash' the sand.

"We can't carry all this wet sand back to your sandpit, Tommy," said Chuckie. "It's too heavy!"

"Let's play with it here then!" said Tommy. Using their seaside buckets and different shaped plastic moulds, the babies used the 'sand' to make lots of pretty sandcastle shapes. Tommy showed the other babies how to fill their buckets and moulds with sand, then turn them upside-down on top of the area that Stu had dug-over.

"Now hit the top of your shapey things - like this!" said Tommy, giving his bucket a thump!

"I've made a starry fish!" laughed Tommy.

"I've made a fish, with big, beady eyeballs!" chuckled Lil.

"I've made a crab, with big, sharp clawers!" grinned Phil.

"I've made a...a...um, big, lumpy...um, rock!" said Chuckie.

"Well, I think you've all made a horrible mess!" said Angelica. "And you're all going to get into big trouble!"

The babies, covered in sand and water, stopped what they were doing and stared at each other.

19

"Angelica's right. We'd better put all the sand back into the sacks," said Chuckie.
The Rugrats didn't know they had mixed sand and cement together. Their shapes were now rock-hard and firmly stuck in the ground!

But when Didi came into the garden, instead of being cross, she looked delighted!
"This looks wonderful!" said Didi, admiring the shapes. "In fact, it looks so good, I can even forgive you babies for getting yourselves so messy!"
"Huh!" muttered Angelica, marching home.
"You babies have saved me a lot of work,"

said Stu, as he painted the figures. "Now I won't have to concrete over this area!"
"No, but you can make some more of those lovely shapes and put them in that area!" said Didi, pointing to another corner of the garden.

"I wouldn't mind a hand with mixing-up some more sand and cement, Deed," said Stu, when the Rugrats had been washed and changed.
"I'd love to help you, Stu, but Betty and I are taking the babies to the park - to play in the sandpit!" laughed Didi.

Sandcastles in the Sun!

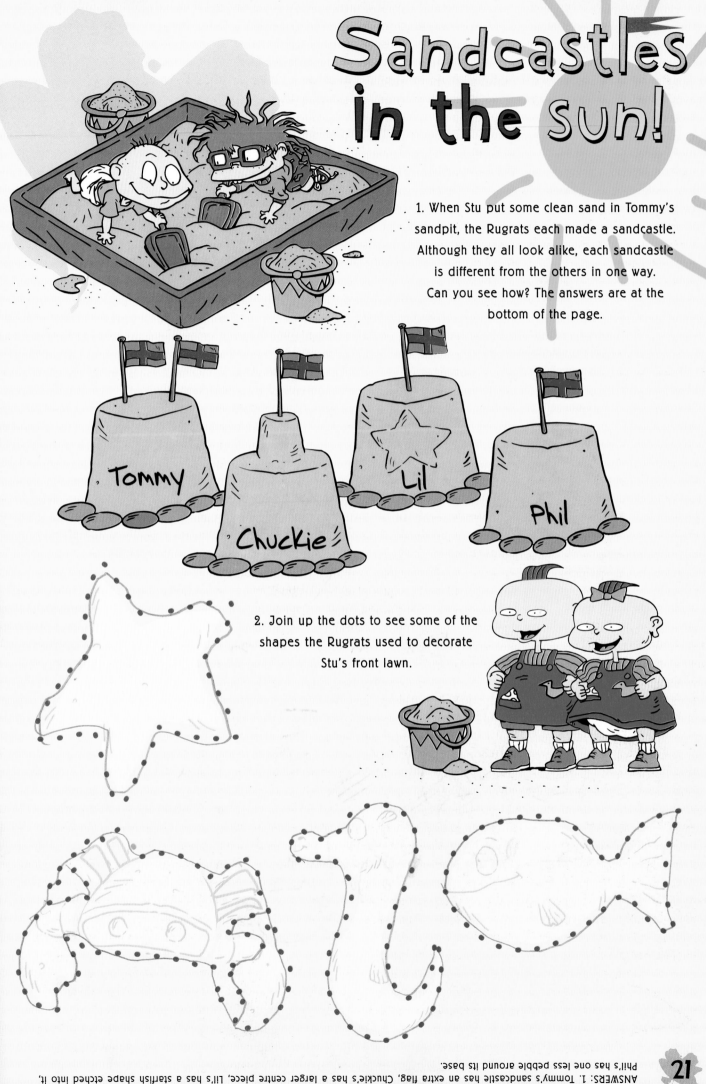

1. When Stu put some clean sand in Tommy's sandpit, the Rugrats each made a sandcastle. Although they all look alike, each sandcastle is different from the others in one way. Can you see how? The answers are at the bottom of the page.

Tommy

Chuckie

Lil

Phil

2. Join up the dots to see some of the shapes the Rugrats used to decorate Stu's front lawn.

ANSWERS: 1. Tommy's sandcastle has an extra flag, Chuckie's has a larger centre piece, Lil's has a starfish shape etched into it, Phil's has one less pebble around its base.

COLOUR CHANGES

Before you colour the top picture of the Rugrats making shapes in the sand, say how picture 'B' is different to 'A' in eight ways. The answers are at the bottom of the page.

24

25

BUZZZZZZY BEES!

Angelica ran for her life when a swarm of angry bees buzzed around her head! Guess which path she should take to reach the Rugrats tent, then trace along that path to see if you are right!

ANSWER: Angelica should take path '2'.

RUGRATS' ALPHA QUIZ

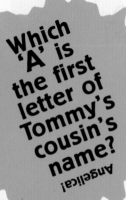

Which 'A' is the first letter of Tommy's cousin's name?

Angelica!

Which 'B' is another name for the Rugrats?

Babies!

Which Rugrat's name begins with 'C'?

Chuckie!

Which 'D' is Tommy's mum's name?

Didi!

Which 'E' is our planet?

Earth!

Which 'F' has five toes?

Foot!

Which 'G' is a large ape?

Gorilla!

Which 'H' grows on top of your head?

Hair!

Which 'K' is a toy you fly in the sky?

Kite!

Which 'J' is a funny story?

Joke!

Which 'I' do Eskimoes live in?

Igloo!

Which 'L' do you do if you find something funny?
Laugh!

Which 'M' is something you use to buy things with?
Money!

Which 'Z' is a striped animal?
A zebra!

Which 'Y' lasts 52 weeks?
A year!

Which 'X' is a picture of the bones of your body?
X-ray!

Which 'W' tells you the time?
A watch!

Which 'V' is something you put flowers into?
A vase!

Which 'N' is at the opposite end of South?
North!

Which 'U' shelters people from the rain?
An umbrella!

Which 'O' is a large sea?
Ocean!

Which 'P' can be a jigsaw or a crossword?
puzzle!

Which 'Q' is the wife of a king?
Queen!

Which 'T' is a slow-moving creature?
A tortoise!

Which 'S' makes things taste sweet?
Sugar!

Which 'R' is a precious red stone?
A ruby!

31

RAINBOW'S END

Grandpa was going to look after the Rugrats while Didi and Betty went shopping.

"How the heck are ya?" boomed Betty, giving Grandpa a friendly pat on the back.

"Fine...cough...just fine!" wheezed Grandpa.

"There's nothing like a good slap on the back to get you up and movin'!"

As Didi searched for her shopping bag, Grandpa prepared to start work on his latest hobby - painting portraits!

"I'll get the Sprouts to pose for me this afternoon," said Grandpa, as Didi and Betty went out.

"Good luck!" called Betty. "If you can get those two kids of mine to sit still long enough, I'll..."

"Stop slapping me on the back?" asked Grandpa, hopefully.

Angelica watched as Grandpa tried to get the Rugrats to keep still. "Huh! You wouldn't catch me posing like that!" Angelica whispered to Cynthia, as Grandpa swished his paintbrush across the paper.

"**M**y daddy's going to take me to a real porterit painter - and he's going to paint a picture of me that's as big as this room!"

Angelica went on. "That's nice," smiled Grandpa.

Angelica was fed up of being ignored. When no one was watching, she took some of

the babies' toys. "Those dumb babies are so busy posing, they won't miss these!" muttered Angelica, sneaking into the back yard.
From an upstairs window, Stu watched as Angelica hid the babies' toys inside a rubbish bin.

Coming dowstairs to see what Angelica was up to, Stu found Grandpa fast asleep in a chair - and the Rugrats splashing paint all over the walls!
"Just what are you babies...?" began Stu, then he noticed Lou's work of art. "Wow! A great painting!" he chuckled.
"Eh, what?..." mumbled Grandpa, stirring from the chair.

"Painting in the style of Picasso, I see!" grinned Stu, not sure which way up the painting should be.
"I'll have you know that that's Lou Pickles' style - and no one else's!" said Grandpa.

Looking around at the rainbow spattered walls, Grandpa said, "I'll tell you Sprouts a story, then clean up this mess while you take a nap!"
The babies listened as Grandpa said,
"Wherever there's a rainbow, you can be sure there's hidden treasure at the end of it..."
Before long, Grandpa's eyelids drooped and he began to snore loudly.
"We could search for the end of a rainbow!"

33

Tommy told Chuckie and the twins.
"Sounds scary, Tommy!" sighed Chuckie. "I mean, how would we even start?"
"By finding the beginning of a rainbow first, I s'pose," said Tommy.

In the back yard, rain fell as Tommy, Chuckie and the twins splashed through muddy puddles.
"I don't like this, Tommy!" wailed Chuckie, as big pear-shaped tears rolled down his cheeks and plopped on to

the ground.
"If you keep crying, you'll make the rainy puddles even bigger - and then you'll fall in one and get covered in water, right up to your nose!" said Tommy.
Chuckie stopped crying at once and made horrible sniffling noises, instead!

"**I** found a rainbow!" called Phil, pointing to a rainbow's reflection in a puddle.
"I don't think that rainbows in puddles count," said Tommy.
"Don't count! Don't count!"

laughed Lil.

"Do too! Do too!" cried Phil.

Just then, Tommy saw a rainbow in the sky.

"Follow me!" he called, racing ahead. Chuckie was so busy looking up at the rainbow, he didn't watch where he was running - and tripped over something on the ground!

"I hurt my l-leg!" sobbed Chuckie, as the others rushed over.

"What's this?" said Lil, sniffing inside a big paper bag, near where Chuckie had fallen.

Tommy ripped open the bag, only to find a pile of smelly potato peelings.

"Yummy!" said Phil, holding up a twisty potato skin.

"Look! We haven't reached the end of the rainbow yet!" said Tommy, pointing towards the sky.

shoved him out of the way and leaped on to the mound of earth.

"Just Spike's smelly old bones!" sighed Tommy, raking over the soggy ground.

After finding an empty cookie jar and a deflated football, the Rugrats decided to give up their search. Then, as they turned to go home, Chuckie let out a loud squeal! "There it is! I saw the end of the rainbow first!" he cheered.

The Rugrats ran to where the rainbow appeared to end - behind the rubbish bin! Right there, Tommy and his friends found a cardboard box, filled with toys!

"These are the bestest treasures in the whole world!" laughed Chuckie, picking up a ball with big red spots on it.

"These are our toys! How did they get here?" said Tommy, puzzled.

What are you babies doing? That's my very privatest box! Put it back right now!" snapped Angelica, as the Rugrats struggled to pull the box over the bumpy ground.

On and on ran the Rugrats, until they saw Spike trying to dig something out of the ground.

"It must be the treasure!" laughed Chuckie, forgetting about his sore leg.

Spike yelped as Tommy, Chuckie, Phil and Lil

"No, I won't, Angelica!" said Tommy. "These are our toys - and you stoled them from us!" A few moments later, Stu appeared. He picked up the toys and took them back to the house. "I wonder how these toys could have got behind that bin?" said Stu. Angelica blushed.

When Didi and Betty returned from their shopping trip, the Rugrats were happily playing with their toys in the play pen.

"Give those toys to me! I want..." began Angelica, as she rushed into the room and grabbed a ball out of Chuckie's hand.

"You were saying, Angelica?" said Stu, coming into the room.

"Um, I was saying that the babies should look after their toys, in case they lose them," mumbled Angelica.

"Mmm, I suppose the toys could get lost, or even thrown away in a rubbish bin!" smiled Stu, knowingly.

"For being such good kids, it's time for a special treat!" announced Betty, taking some Reptar bars out of her shopping bag.

"I-I'll help you to put away the shopping, Auntie Didi," said Angelica, trying not to look at Stu.

"Now, who deserves one of these?" asked Stu, holding up the Reptar Bars. As Tommy, Chuckie and the twins eagerly reached out for their treats, Angelica hung her head.

"Where's your Reptar bar, Angelica?" asked Chuckie, between mouthfuls.

"Why don't you look for the rainbow's end, Angelica?" laughed Tommy. "You might find a lishus Reptar bar there!"

The **Rugrats** are following a rainbow, to see if it leads them to Tommy's toybox! To play this game with friends, you will each need different coloured counters. Place your counters on 'start' and take turns to throw a dice. Whichever number appears, move that many spaces. If you land on a coloured space, look at the matching coloured rainbow - and do what the message tells you.

The first to reach 'finish' wins!

15   14   13   12

16

17

RED GO ON 2 SPACES

PINK GO BACK 4 SPACES

18   19   20   21   22

RUGRATS

39   38   37   36

40

41

BLUE GO BACK 2 SPACES

INDIGO GO ON 4 SPACES

42   43   44   45   46   4

1 START
2
3
4
5
10
9
8
7
6

YELLOW
MISS A TURN

GREEN
GO BACK
TO START

24
25
26
27
28
29

RAINBOW

34
33
32
31
30

VIOLET
TAKE AN
EXTRA GO

48
49
50 FINISH

TOY BOX

RUGRATS RAINBOW CAKE

**The Rugrats' favourite food
is Rainbow cake. With a grown-up's help,
you can have fun making a rainbow cake, too!**

1

First line a cake tin with clingfilm and cover the base with crushed biscuits. Then put in as many different coloured scoops of ice-cream as you can and press down well.

2

Scoop some ice-cream out of the centre of the tin, then pour drained fruit into the hollow, almost to the top. Replace the scooped out ice-cream and then freeze until firm.

3

To remove the cake from the mould, press the bottom of the cake tin on to a tin can.

4

Hold a plate over the top of the cake tin and turn it over. Then remove the 'cake' from the base and take off the clingfilm. Now decorate the top with fresh fruit and it's ready to eat. Scrummy!

Down The Drain!

Tommy was having a great time splashing around in the bath. Then something caught his eye. As Didi fixed a loose screw on the bathroom cabinet, Tommy leaned towards the shiny object - and tugged it hard!

Tilting his head, Tommy listened as a loud sucking noise erupted...then the water began to swirl round and round! As his little toy soldier was sucked into the whirlpool, Tommy watched, fascinated. With a final GLURP! the soldier disappeared down the plug hole. "Oh, Tommykins, did something scare you?" asked Didi, as Tommy burst into tears.

Next morning, Didi dropped Tommy and Angelica off at Chuckie's house.
"Thanks for taking care of the kids, Charles," said Didi. Chaz looked at the diapers, toys and bottles that Didi had put down. There were enough to last Tommy a week!
As Tommy and Angelica raced into the house, Didi looked thoughtful.
"Oh, one other

thing, Charles," she whispered. "Tommy's going through his Water Rejection Stage!"
"Don't worry. If there's one thing I know, it's how to get a kid to take a bath!" smiled Chaz. "Trust me, Deed."

Later, Tommy broke into loud sobs as he explained his fear of baths to Chuckie. "I used to be the same...until a voice told me the truth!" said Chuckie, switching on his toy cassette player. Suddenly, a voice sang:
The water's your friend,
The bath is your pal,
You can't get sucked down the drain.
Don't worry, don't worry...

"So you kids are scared of goin' down the drain, huh?" scoffed Angelica. "Well, you should be! That dumb old song is a big fib! A course you can go down the drain!" She walked over to the door and looked back at the babies.

"Suckers! They bought it!" she grinned, leaving the room.
"What're we gonna do, Tommy?" sobbed Chuckie.
At last, Tommy came up with a plan. While Chaz practised his 'Don't be afraid of the water' voice and wiggled two hand puppets, Tommy and Chuckie crept into the bathroom.

With the help of a few tubs of clay-dough, Tommy filled in the plug hole. Turning on the taps, they watched as the tub filled. "Neat!" grinned Angelica, as bubbles of clay dough burped up from the plug hole. Then in a loud voice, Angelica yelled, "MR. FINSTER! COME LOOK WHAT THE BABIES HAS DONE!" Charles ran into the bathroom just in time to see water cascading over the sides of the bath!

As Tommy and Chuckie sat in the back yard, waiting for the plumber to dig out the last pieces of clay dough, Angelica came along. "Nice try, babies, but you failed!" she grinned.

Throwing sand from the sandpit into the air, Angelica went on, "Too bad you can't bath in sand instead of water, don'tcha think? 'Cos sand is so easy to move. You can take it anywhere!" As he watched Angelica, Tommy had another idea. He and Chuckie waited for the plumber to leave, then crept back into the bathroom, carrying little buckets of sand.

After several trips to the sandpit, the plug hole was blocked again.

"Aha, here you guys are!" called Chaz, waving his hand puppets in the air. "I'd like you to meet Mr. Water and Mr. Dirty! They... ARGHHHH!"

Tommy and Chuckie watched as the plumber arrived a second time. Meanwhile, Angelica was busy talking to her doll. "Isn't this a great jacuzzi, Cynthia?" Angelica grinned, looking down into the toilet. "Want me to turn on the bubbles? Okay!"

"There it is, Chuckie!" groaned Tommy, pointing to the bath. "After tonight, we'll be gone!"

"Too bad!" grinned Angelica.

Angelica was still laughing as she flushed the toilet. The vibration violently rocked Cynthia from the seat.

"That's funny, eh, Cynthia?" whispered Angelica. "CYNTHIA?"

Angelica screamed and screamed! Cynthia had fallen down the toilet - and disappeared!

The plumber was called out for the third time!

"Oh, please let Cynthia be okay!" Angelica sobbed, as the plumber took the entire toilet apart. At last, he handed her the bent and beaten doll.

Clutching her broken doll, Angelica was still sobbing when Drew came to take her home.

"It's true! You can get sucked down the drain!" Angelica wailed.

"We're doomed, Tommy!" sighed Chuckie.

"Oh, boys...iiiiiittt's BATH TIME!" called Chaz, in his high-pitched puppet voice.

Terrified, Tommy and Chuckie looked at each other...and ran!

"What did I say?" sighed Charles.

At last, Chaz managed to get Tommy and Chuckie into the bath. "See, you guys, the water's not scary. The water is your friend...Well, actually, it's just a random collection of molecules, but..." The ringing phone interrupted him in mid-flow.

Telling Tommy and Chuckie to sit still, Charles went to answer the phone.
"I'm goin' down there, Chuckie," stammered Tommy, staring at the plug hole.
"Hey, you don't have to go down there. The drain's all plugged up and our bath's almost over!" gasped Chuckie.
"But what about tomorrow's bath...and the bath after that?" sighed Tommy. "Am I gonna be afraid forever?"
Tommy took a deep breath, then before he could change his mind, he gave the chain a big tug! The sound of sucking water filled the room...and nothing happened! Bravely, Tommy put his foot over the drain. The vibration of the sucking water just tickled!

"Hey, this is great!" Tommy giggled, sitting on top of the drain. "I'm tickling all over!"
When Didi and Charles came into the room, Tommy and Chuckie were playing with the swirling water as it whooshed towards the drain.
"You did it, Charles!" laughed Didi.
"I did?" said Charles.
"You are an expert! You cured Tommy of his water phobia!" Didi went on.
Wiggling his hand puppets and using a funny voice, Chaz said, "Gee, thanks!"

45

JUST JOKING!

These are some of the rib-tickling jokes that make the Rugrats laugh
How many jokes can you read without bursting into laughter, too?

Which fish sings?
A tuna fish!

How do you make toast in a jungle?
Under a gorilla!

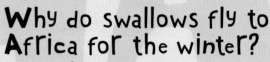

LETTUCE IN!

What did James Bond catch after his latest mission?
A code in the nose!

Why do giraffes have long necks?
Because they have smelly feet!

Why do swallows fly to Africa for the winter?
Because it's too far to walk!

How does a flea get from one place to another?
By itch-hiking!

How do you stop moles digging in your garden?
Take away their spades!

What do short-sighted ghosts wear?
Spoookticals!

How do elephants talk to each other?
On elephones!

Which bird always succeeds?
A bird with no teeth!

Why do bees have sticky hair?
Because they use honey combs!

What is small, white and laughs a lot?
A tickled onion!

If cheese comes after pudding, what comes after cheese?
A mouse!

What do you give an injured lemon?
Lemonade!

What do sea monsters eat?
Fish and ships!

What did the sea say to the sand?
Nothing. He just waved!

How do you send a baby astronaut to sleep?
Rocket!

What fish wears spurs and a cowboy hat?
Billy the cod!

Who never minds being interrupted in the middle of a sentence?
A prisoner!

WHERE'S ANGELICA?

Room 5

Room 10

Angelica is hiding behind one of these doors - but which one? Find out by solving the maths problem for the Rugrats, so that they can miss Angelica and go through the door where she has hidden their toys! The answer is at the bottom of the page.

Key:

 means =

 means +

 means -

 means 1

 means 2

 means 3

 means 4

48

YOU CAN DO MAGIC!

I can pick up the marble inside that jar, without touching anything except the jar!

Can you work out how Angelica did it?

How can Phil and Lil get rid of the middle card, without moving it?

How can Tommy do that?

All the answers are at the bottom of the page.

I can lift an ice cube out of that glass of water with this piece of string!

ANSWERS: Marble trick: hold the jar and quickly turn it round and move up the jar. Quickly turn the jar over, so the marble drops to the bottom - and you can pick it up. Ice cube trick: sprinkle salt on the ice cube, then lay the string on the ice and wait for a few seconds. Lift up the string - and the ice will come with it! Card trick: take away one of the side cards - and there is no middle one left!

Angelica Misbehives!

The Rugrats' parents decided to 'get back to the simple life', by taking a camping vacation.

"Breakfast will be ready soon!" called Stu, as he and Drew prepared food on a griddle.

"I'm hungry!" whispered Chuckie, peering out of the tent.

"Mmm, whatever Dad's cooking, it smells..." began Tommy. Suddenly, there was a loud CRASH!

"Um, breakfast might be a little longer than I thought!" called Stu.

The portable table had collapsed on to the muddy ground, taking all the food with it!

"Oh, nooo!" sobbed Chuckie. "Now we won't have anything to eat!"

"What was that?" asked Phil, when he heard a rumbling noise.

"It's my tummy, Phillip!" said Lil. "It's telling me it's empty!"

"I see food!" chuckled Phil, leaping on some biscuit crumbs that had stuck to a blanket.

"I saw them first, Phillip!" cried Lil, leaping on top of her brother.

As the twins rolled around on the ground, Chuckie let out a cry.

"Look what I've found!" he grinned. "A big jar of honey!"

But Chuckie stopped laughing when he peered inside the jar. It was empty!

"I know where honey comes from!" sang Angelica, coming into the Rugrats' tent.
"So do I!" said Tommy. "It comes from the big store in town!"
"Huh! You don't know anything!" laughed Angelica. "Honey comes from bees...and I know where some bees live! I'm going to get some honey to eat now!" she declared, creeping out of the back of the tent.
"I knowed where there's a napple tree and big napples grow on it!" said Tommy. "If you share your honey, Angelica, I'll showed you where the napple tree is!"

Reluctantly, Angelica agreed. As they scrambled through a bush, Tommy pointed to an apple tree. But Angelica had no intention of trying to climb the tree herself!
"Crouch down on the ground and let Tommy climb on to your back, Chuckie!" said Angelica, in her bossiest voice. "Then Tommy can reach some of the apples."
"I think I'm g-going to bend, Tommy!" cried Chuckie, wobbling from side to side.

As Chuckie lost his balance and rolled over, Tommy grabbed a tree branch.
"Heeeelp!" cried Chuckie, as apples fell from the tree, hitting the Rugrats.
"Dumb babies!" laughed Angelica.

57

But when Angelica picked up the fruit, she saw that it was all bruised. "If you babies want honey, you'll have to get it yourselves!" she cried, as Tommy rubbed his head. When Angelica marched off in a huff, the Rugrats followed. "I don't knowed everything like you, Angelica," said Tommy, "but I knowed that bees sting!" "Look! There aren't any bees here!" said Angelica, pointing to the bees' hive. "Now go get some honey!" The Rugrats looked at each other and shook their heads. "Scared, huh?" called

Angelica. "Well, you can all go back to the tent, scaredy-cats! I'll get the honey - and eat it all myself!"

"My tummy is talking again, Tommy!" moaned Phil, as his tummy made a loud gurgling noise.

"My tummy's talking more than yours, Phillip!" cried Lil.

"Is not!" argued Phil.

"I'm too hungry to argue, even if I wanted to!" gulped Chuckie.

As the Rugrats walked back to their tent, Angelica slowly moved towards the bees' hive, hanging from a tree.

"I'm not afraid of silly little bees!" she mumbled, looking nervously around her.

Just then, Drew came into the Rugrats' tent, carrying a huge jar of honey.

"Look what I bought from the farm shop!" smiled Drew, holding out the jar for Angelica to taste. "Your favourite - honey!"

"Don't mention that word!" cried Angelica, holding her hands to her ears. "I don't like that nasty stuff!"

Suddenly, a bee appeared and buzzed around Angelica's head. Flicking it away with one hand, Angelica moved a little closer. Then a second bee swooped down...then a third...then more and more!
"Wait for meeee!" cried Angelica, as she turned and ran, the bees flying close behind.

By the time Angelica got back to the tent, the Rugrats were happily eating honey on bread.
"How did you get that honey?" gasped Angelica, looking behind her to make sure there were no bees still following.

The grown-ups looked at each other with puzzled expressions.
"That's strange, I thought you liked H-O-N-E-Y!" said Drew, spelling out the word.
Angelica's cheeks flushed a bright pink as the Rugrats looked at each other and smiled, knowingly.

"You'll all have to be careful," Drew told everyone. "On my way to the farm, I spotted a bee hive not far from here!"

"I could have told them that!" muttered Angelica, as the grown-ups walked away.

Angelica was so hungry, she could have eaten almost anything!

"Don't you have anything else to eat?" Angelica asked the Rugrats, in her sweetest voice.

"Well..." said Tommy, between mouthfuls of gooey bread. "We did have some bananas that Uncle Drew gave us!"

"Give me one!" cried Angelica, licking her lips.

"We did have some, Angelica" said Tommy, "but we ated them all!"

Stu and Drew decided it would be safer to camp somewhere else.

So later that day, while the grown-ups sat inside their tent and sang songs, the Rugrats played nearby.

The grown-ups had erected their tent in Stu and Didi's back yard!

Sitting in a corner of the yard, Angelica kept looking around her, just to make sure there were no bees close by.

"What are you looking for, honey?" asked Drew.

"Why does everyone keep saying that word?" Angelica groaned.

WHAT DO YOU KNOW?

How much do you really know about the Rugrats?
To find out, answer the questions below and write the answers in the correct spaces.
Some letters have already been written to help you.

CLUES:
1. She helps Tommy to solve his problems
2. Susie Carmichael's mom
3. Tommy's dad
4. Tommy's dog
5. Lillian's twin
6. Stu's wife
7. She and Phillip always argue
8. Chuckie's best friend
9. Tommy's favourite dinosaur
10. Lucy Carmichael's husband
11. He tells stories to the Rugrats
12. Stu's brother
13. She likes to boss the Rugrats around
14. Didi is Angelica's ...
15. The twins' mom
16. It doesn't take much to make him cry
17. The twins' dad
18. Angelica's doll
19. Stu is Drew's ...

61

IT'S A BULLSEYE!

Tommy, Chuckie and Angelica had a great time throwing toy darts at dart boards. Tommy scored 45 points, Chuckie scored 35 points and Angelica scored 40 points. Each player got all three of their darts in different numbered sections on their target. Can you colour in the circles that had darts in them?